Washington Irving's

ICHABOD CRANE
AND THE HEADLESS HORSEMAN

retold by
Carol Beach York

illustrated by
Diana Uehlinger

Folk Tales of America

Troll Associates

PROLOGUE

On the quiet banks of the Hudson River in New York, Washington Irving first wrote the tale of Ichabod Crane and the Headless Horseman.

This tale of ghosts and terror takes place in Sleepy Hollow—a village as quiet as its name.

Although the hero, Ichabod, was not strong or brave, like so many other American folk heroes, his story has been handed down to us over the years.

Just as the stories told by the villagers of Sleepy Hollow made life just a bit more exciting, Ichabod's tale shows how the power of imagination and story-telling can spice up our own everyday lives.

Copyright © 1980 by Troll Associates

Library of Congress# 79-66323
ISBN 0-89375-316-5/0-89375-315-7 (pb)

10 9 8 7 6 5 4 3

Ichabod Crane was the schoolmaster in a quiet little village called Sleepy Hollow.

The title of "Schoolmaster" sounds very grand. It certainly sounded grand to Ichabod Crane when he was hired.

But the schoolhouse was only one room, made of logs. It stood in the quiet woods by a brook, not a very exciting spot. Ichabod was a little disappointed when he first saw it.

He decorated his desk with inkpots and quill pens and books. He sat on a high stool with his heels hooked over a rung. As the children endlessly recited their lessons, Ichabod wondered if he was going to like Sleepy Hollow.

The peaceful valley was shaded by walnut
and birch trees. The Hudson River was only a
few miles away. None of the bustle of the mar-
ket towns along the river disturbed the
drowsy, lazy days of Sleepy Hollow. One day
was quite like the next. The brook trickled
along. The church bell rang on Sunday. Bees
drifted over the flowers in the warm sun.

But Ichabod soon discovered that Sleepy Hollow was not as dull as he first thought.

The people who lived there—sturdy farm families—spiced up their lives with tales of ghosts and goblins. They spoke of spirits that haunted side roads, and of demons hidden in the woods. In fact, they told such frightening, nightmarish stories that Ichabod began to believe he had come to live in the most bewitched valley in all the world.

As schoolmaster, Ichabod boarded at different farmhouses. He lived a week at one house, a week at another. And he heard the stories of demons and goblins at every fireside—so much so that he began to dread being out after dark! Trees became ghosts in the moonlight. A night owl's cry was a screaming witch.

The most popular of all Sleepy Hollow tales was the story of a mysterious rider who roamed the woods at night on a fast, dark horse.

That was scary enough.

But the rider had no head! And this, of course, made him all the scarier.

The story said that this grim rider had been a soldier in the Revolutionary War, a war that was not long past. His head had been shot off by a cannonball. The rest of him had been buried in the church graveyard. At night his ghost galloped about the countryside, looking for his missing head.

The people of Sleepy Hollow never tired of telling this story.

"He has to be back to the graveyard before daybreak," the storyteller would say.

"What if he isn't?" the children would ask, their eyes wide with fear.

No one knew the answer to that.

"Never mind," the storyteller would say. "He just *has* to be. He rides like a whirlwind. If you're in the woods before light, you can hear the hoofbeats thundering as he dashes back to the grave."

None of the children were in the woods before light. But if they had been, they wouldn't have wanted to meet the rider. He was known as the Headless Horseman of Sleepy Hollow.

With all these horrifying tales told around the fire, Ichabod Crane began to think that Sleepy Hollow was rather exciting after all.

And to add to the excitement, he fell in love.

You see, the job of Sleepy Hollow school-master didn't pay very much. So Ichabod took the spare-time job of singing master. He led the songs at church and gave singing lessons to the young ladies. Katrina Van Tassel was one of the young ladies. Ichabod Crane fell in love with her the moment he saw her.

Katrina was a pretty, pink-cheeked girl.

To make things even better, her father was very rich.

Ichabod, struggling along on his skimpy salary, loved to visit the Van Tassel farm. Luxuries were everywhere. The house was finely furnished, and the barnyard was full of fat pigs and strutting turkeys. The trees in the orchards were heavy with fruit. Fields of corn and wheat stretched into the distance.

Ichabod would sit at his school desk and daydream of the time he would marry Katrina and perhaps one day inherit the Van Tassel wealth as well.

The only flaw in his daydream was that Katrina had another beau. She could not decide between her two suitors.

The other fellow was a big, sturdy young man named Brom Van Brunt. Because he was so big and strong, he was nicknamed Brom Bones. No one could beat him in a fight or outride him on a horse. As if this weren't enough, he was also very handsome, with curly black hair and a cheery smile. A fine young man, indeed.

Ichabod Crane, on the other hand, was as thin as a beanpole, with a bird-beak nose and a skinny neck. He had such long arms and legs that he seemed to be made entirely of knees and elbows. His sleeves and trousers were never quite long enough. He had never once been in a fight, and he could barely stay on a horse.

But Ichabod had read ever so many books. Katrina admired that. She thought it was a feather in her cap to be courted by the village schoolmaster.

15

Now, Brom had known Katrina first, and he wasn't going to let her go easily. So it was not long before Ichabod was in trouble.

During one of Ichabod's singing lessons, someone got on the roof and stuffed up the chimney. All the young ladies had to run outside to escape the smoky room. Ichabod piled his arms with singing books and came stumbling after. The whole lesson was ruined.

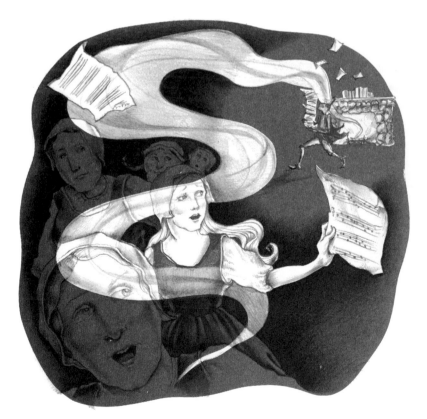

Another time, Ichabod found that someone had sneaked into the schoolhouse at night, spilled the inkpots, and turned the desks upside-down. His high stool was missing. He found it in the woods some days later, with a squirrel sitting on top of it cracking nuts.

"It's that naughty Brom Bones playing tricks on you," Katrina comforted Ichabod. "You ought to whip him good."

Fight Brom Bones? Ichabod didn't think much of that idea. Brom Bones would flatten him with one blow.

"But aren't you angry?" Katrina's pretty blue eyes were blazing.

"Oh, no. He's just having a little fun," Ichabod said. He pretended to laugh. "Good old Brom. Ha ha ha."

Ichabod tried to think of some trick he could play on Brom Bones. No trick came to mind, but he didn't give up. He was sitting at his school desk one day trying to think of a trick, when a servant boy rode up from the Van Tassel farm. Ichabod Crane was invited to a party at the Van Tassel house that evening.

This delightful invitation drove everything else from Ichabod's head. He could hardly wait for evening to come. He began to think of what he would wear.

The children were having a reading lesson, but Ichabod scarcely heard a thing. They began to wriggle at their desks. They began to whisper and giggle.

"Quiet there," Ichabod said absently. His mind was on the party. He had only one good suit—he would have to wear that.

"Next child." He roused long enough to look for a new reader. It was a barefoot lad who hardly knew one word from another.

"Fine, fine." Ichabod nodded absent-mindedly. "Next child."

Then Ichabod dismissed school an hour early and raced up the road to get ready for the party.

Ichabod's one good suit was no longer so very good. He brushed it until it nearly fell apart. At last he put it on, and he buttoned up the coat. He fussed with the cuffs and collar. He fussed with the coattails and pockets. He admired himself in the mirror. He was ready.

Ichabod was boarding at this time with a crabby old farmer named Hans Van Ripper. When Ichabod had arranged his cuffs and collar one last time, he went downstairs. Van Ripper was smoking his pipe in the kitchen. He didn't know Ichabod had been primping for a party all this time. He thought the school-teacher looked about the same as ever—long and scrawny and all knees and elbows.

"Would it be possible to borrow your horse?" Ichabod asked politely.

Van Ripper wasn't keen on this. His horse wasn't much, but he didn't like lending things.

"I'm invited to a party at the Van Tassels'," Ichabod explained. He smoothed a cuff.

Van Ripper grumbled a bit longer, but in the end he went to the barn with Ichabod. The old horse was resting. It had not been expecting any more activity that day.

"It's a new saddle," Van Ripper grumbled.

"I'll be very careful with it," Ichabod promised.

The stirrups were too short for him, and his knees stuck up. Old Gunpowder was blind in one eye and his mane was straggly and tangled. But Ichabod rode off feeling like a king. His coattails flew out behind, and he nearly lost his hat on the first roadside tree branch. Van Ripper had a good laugh at the sight. Then he went back to his pipe.

It was a fine autumn day. Ichabod bounced
along on the one-eyed horse through the
golden woods. Birds twittered in the trees.
Rays of setting sun streaked the grassy slopes
of the valley and spread a pink glow across the
cloudless sky. Ah, it was a wonderful, wonderful day. And here was he, Ichabod Crane, on
his way to his beloved, wearing a fine suit, rid-
ing a fine horse.

"Tonight I'll propose to Katrina," he said to himself.

He admired his reflection in the brook, and then rode on.

At the Van Tassel farm, the party had already begun. Valley farmers had put a shine to their shoe buckles. Farm wives wore their Sunday-best lace caps. Such finery Ichabod had never seen. He tied up the old horse and made his way to the main parlor.

There is more to a party than fine clothes. Ichabod learned that right away. In fact, he thought he was in heaven when he caught sight of the refreshment table.

Pumpkin pies, peach pies, smoked hams.

A shank of beef, a roast of pork.

Honey cakes, apple cider, bowls of cheese, and platters of chicken.

Warm breads and plum jam.

Ichabod did not know where to start. But he plunged right in.

Outside, Brom Bones dashed up on his horse, Daredevil, a beast so wild that no one else in the valley could ride him.

"Brom Bones! Brom Bones!" A cheer went up—along with clouds of dust—as Brom flashed into the yard on his splendid, fiery steed.

Ichabod was too busy eating to notice.

He especially liked the juicy beef. Honey cakes melted in his mouth.

Katrina's father moved among the guests, slapping shoulders, shaking hands. "Eat, eat," he urged.

Ichabod Crane needed no urging. He fixed himself a second plate.

When the dancing began, Ichabod stopped
eating and led Katrina onto the floor. He
flopped and flapped around as the fiddler
scraped his bow over the strings.

Brom Bones stood in a corner and frowned.

"Ichabod stole your sweetheart, eh, Brom?"
one of his friends said with a grin.

Brom didn't answer.

The old farmers gathered in a corner. They lit up their pipes and talked about the Revolutionary War. The war was not far gone, but far gone enough for the details to be fuzzy. Each farmer seemed to be the hero of his own story. But it was not long before the story-telling turned to the goblins and the ghosts and the scary things that haunted Sleepy Hollow.

"Now you take the woman in white," a stout old farmer said. His listeners nodded. They knew the story well. The poor woman had lost her way and died in a snowstorm. Her ghost haunted dark places and startled travelers in the night.

"I saw her myself just two days ago in the glen at Raven Rock."

"Ohhhhh." The listeners shuddered with horrible delight.

"Shrieking, she was. Shrieking to raise the dead."

"Ohhhh." The listeners shivered again. Puffs of pipe smoke rose to the ceiling. Heads nodded. The woman in white was a thing to be reckoned with, indeed.

But as always, the favorite story was the story of the Headless Horseman.

"He's not been about of late," someone said.

"You're wrong!" a voice spoke up. "I saw him near the churchyard myself, not a week ago."

There was a moment of silence. Then someone said, "And you're here today?"

"Aye, I'm here today. I hid behind a tree. He rode right by, near enough to touch. But he didn't see me."

"Your good luck," the other farmers agreed.

The dancing ended, and Ichabod joined the pipe smokers in the quiet corner. The tales they told there in the shadows were like real life to him. He could almost hear the loud sound of hoofbeats when the Headless Horseman galloped back to the churchyard as the first pale light of dawn stained the sky.

And then a loud voice said, "Bah, he's nothing to worry about!"

Every head turned.

It was Brom Bones. Big and sturdy and strong.

"I met him one night," Brom said. *Ohs* and *ahs* went around the room. Ichabod pricked up his ears.

"He tried to race me," Brom said.

Every head was bent toward Brom. Every ear was listening.

"I'd have beaten him." Brom strutted about. "Daredevil and I would have beaten him."

The listeners nodded. They knew Daredevil was the fastest horse in all Sleepy Hollow.

"We were going along neck and neck." Brom lowered his voice to a whisper. "Till we came to the church bridge."

Every head bent closer. Farmers cupped their hands to their ears, so they wouldn't miss a word.

"And then what?" a small trembling voice asked.

Brom waited a moment. No one breathed. Ichabod felt his heart thump at the thought of meeting the Headless Horseman.

"Till we came to the church bridge," Brom repeated. "And then—"

"And then?" The old farmers let their pipes hang loose in their mouths.

"And then he vanished in a flash of fire."

"A flash of fire?"

"Aye," Brom said. "A flash of fire. Puff—he was gone!"

Ichabod Crane felt a cold chill creeping along his skinny arms. He felt his limp, scraggly hair rising on his head. He thought of the long, dark ride back to Van Ripper's house. A long, dark ride through the lonesome woods.

The lively party had changed now. Ichabod no longer felt so joyful, so blissfully happy. The golden woods where he had ridden were dark and shadowy now. His way home was a dangerous road, traveled by witches and goblins . . . traveled perhaps by the Headless Horseman himself.

"Eat, eat," Van Tassel urged. The fiddler struck up another tune. But Ichabod didn't want to fill another plate or dance another jig.

He did, however, speak to Katrina once again. And then, with a sadly lowered head, he woke up the one-eyed horse, stuck his feet into the short stirrups, and headed down the road.

A midnight moon gave the woods a pale, deathly light. Every tree became a monster with twenty arms. Branches rubbing in the wind made ghostly groans. Fallen leaves rustled like the whispering of witches. Ichabod prodded Gunpowder to a quick trot. He could not get home fast enough!

At last he saw the brook ahead. It was not so far now to Van Ripper's farm. The brook shimmered in the white moonlight—but what was that half-hidden by the trees? A huge, shadowy form stood motionless, waiting.

The poor old horse came to a stop, trembling and shivering.

The dark form did not move.

Ichabod's mouth was dry. His heart hammered.

"Who's there?" he called in a quavering voice.

There was no reply.

Ichabod dug his heels into the ribs of his horse, and the dark shape moved out from the trees.

Ichabod could see now that it was a rider on a black horse. A *headless* rider.

Ichabod took his whip to his terrified horse, and with a bound they crossed the brook.

But the headless rider was close behind. And as Ichabod looked back in panic, he saw that the rider carried his head in front of him on the saddle!

This was too much. Ichabod dug his heels harder and begged his horse to hurry. He closed his eyes and said his prayers. Cold sweat streamed down his face.

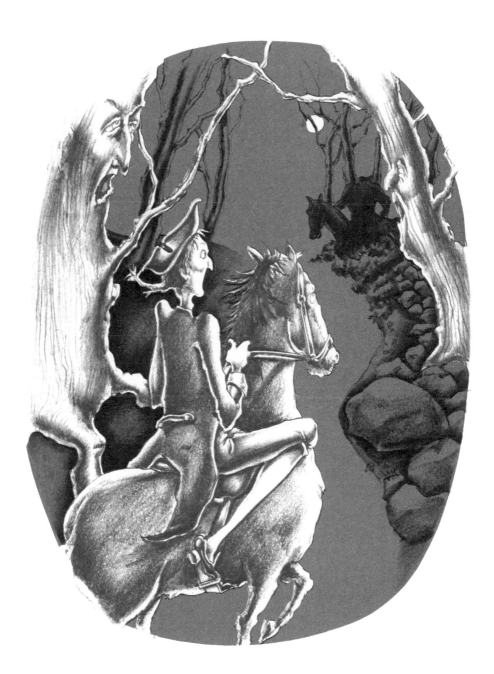

Faster and faster he urged the horse on. Old
Gunpowder ran as though demons were after
him. The Headless Horseman followed just as
fast. Ichabod could hear the pounding hoofbeats close behind.

Ichabod lashed with his whip again. Worn
and saggy as Gunpowder was, he sprang
ahead with a burst of energy and fear. Ichabod
could hardly stay on. And then, to make mat-
ters worse, he felt the saddle slipping. Van
Ripper's new saddle!

Slipping . . . slipping . . . *gone*.

Ichabod heard the saddle thud on the road behind him. A moment later he heard the crushing hooves of the great horse trample over it.

Gunpowder raced along. Ichabod hung on for dear life. His arms were wrapped around the horse's neck, and he slid from side to side, his coattails flying in the wind. The other horse was gaining. Ichabod could feel its hot breath upon his back.

The church loomed ahead, outlined against the moonlit sky. Ichabod cast a desperate glance behind him to see if the rider would vanish in a flash of fire.

No such luck.

The headless rider leaned forward and lifted his head in his hands. His cloak billowed around him. Then, as Ichabod looked back in terror, the rider threw the head straight at him.

Ichabod hunched down, but the flying head hit him hard and knocked him to the ground. The one-eyed horse flew on. The black horse flew on. Hoofbeats rang and screamed through the night, echoed in the distance, and faded away in the darkness.

The next morning Van Ripper found his horse at his gate. Where his best saddle was, the cranky old farmer could not tell. He stormed back into his house to ask Ichabod Crane about it. But Ichabod was not in his bed. The bed had not been slept in all night.

Ichabod did not turn up at the schoolhouse either. The children played outside all morning, but Ichabod Crane never came.

In fact, Ichabod Crane was never seen in Sleepy Hollow again.

Van Ripper did at last find his saddle. A sad mess! And he found Ichabod's hat lying in the dusty road.

Nearby the hat he found—*a smashed pumpkin.*

Some people said Ichabod Crane had gone away because Katrina turned him down on the night of the party.

She married Brom Bones by and by.

Brom always had a sly smile on his face when anyone mentioned the strange disappearance of Ichabod Crane.

Some of the old farmers thought that the Headless Horseman had caught Ichabod— perhaps to borrow his head. They said Ichabod Crane's ghost haunted the woods by the schoolhouse. They said they heard it moaning in the night among the trees.

People say that even now, at night, you can sometimes hear hoofbeats by the churchyard in Sleepy Hollow. Perhaps it is the Headless Horseman, still galloping to catch the ghost of Ichabod Crane.